DENNIS the MENACE

THE MENACE MACHINE!

BEANObooks

published under licence by

meadowside
CHILDREN'S BOOKS

"The Beano" ®©, "Dennis the Menace" ®©
and "Gnasher" ®© D.C. Thomson & Co., Ltd., 2006

THE DENNISBOT

There had been some very strange noises coming from the shed all day. There had been some peculiar smells and several puffs of red and black smoke. Mum and Dad had been trying to pretend that they hadn't noticed anything, but it wasn't easy.

Dad was polishing his golf clubs and reading an article from his favourite magazine, *Which Tie?*, out loud.

Mum was painting her toenails and playing music (*Fifty Cardigan Crooners*) to drown out the sound of Dad blithering on about ties.

Bea was sitting in the kitchen sink and peering out at the garden shed.

At last, they heard something.

"Brilliant!" Dennis's voice chortled. "I'm a genius!"

Mum and Dad looked at each other.

"It's not too late to leave the country," said Dad.

In the shed, Dennis was rubbing his hands together. Gnasher was grinning the sort of grin that had made all the local cats move to Australia.

"This is gonna take menacing onto a whole new level!" Dennis said. "I can do double the amount!" He gazed with pride on his creation.

In the middle of the shed stood a figure wearing a red-and-black striped jumper, a pair of black boots and a spiky black wig.

"It's the Dennisbot!" Dennis explained. "A totally robotic, completely awesome second *me*! I can train him to do anything I want! All I have to do is turn the key in his back to 'in training', and he'll learn how to do everything I show him!"

"Gnassshhhh?" said Gnasher. His grin got even wider.

"When he's learned everything, I just switch the key to 'Menace' and off he goes!" Dennis continued. "Two top menaces in Beanotown! No one can stop me now!"

He walked around the back of the Dennisbot and turned the key to 'In Training', then pulled out the key and grinned at Gnasher.

Just then, they heard Mum's voice.

"Dennis! I've got to bake fifty pies for the charity pie sale!" she bawled from the back door. "Will you look after Bea for an hour?"

"Fifty pies?" said Dennis. "I'd better check this out!"

He pounded out of the shed and up the garden path, with Gnasher at his heels. The shed door swung open on its hinges as Dennis ran into the kitchen.

The Dennisbot's eyes clicked open.

"Out?" it repeated Dennis's last word.

It moved towards the open shed door.

Half an hour later, Dennis was still in the kitchen, leaning against the table with his arms folded.

"I'll just stay here while you cook," he said. "Help you make sure the pies are all tasty enough."

"Oh yes?" said Mum, putting her hands on her hips. "Just like the day you 'helped' me bake cakes for the school fair? I ended up with five crumbs to sell!"

"You got five pence for them!" Dennis chortled. "They filled Walter the Softy's tiny tummy!"

"Dennis, take your little sister out until I have made these pies!" Mum yelled. Dennis scooped Bea up under one arm with a chuckle.

"Okay, okay, I've got training to do anyway."

"Training?" said Mum, suspiciously.

"See you later!" Dennis said, marching out of the back door.

Mum put her hand up to her forehead.

"Don't ask," she told herself faintly. "Just *don't ask*!"

"Right!" said Dennis, striding back into the shed and grinning at the thought of the menacing ahead. "Let's get you started, Dennisbot. First we're gonna – WHERE ARE YOU?"

Gnasher nearly choked on his sausages. The Dennisbot was gone!

Dennis pounded down the street, with Bea under his arm and Gnasher beside him. Up ahead, Curly and Pie Face were fighting over a large pasty. When they saw Dennis their mouths fell open and they dropped the pasty (Gnasher wolfed it down before they realised).

"How did you do that?" gasped Curly.

"What?" Dennis growled. "Never mind that, this is an emergency!"

"BOT!" shouted Bea.

"But – but – but you just went past!" Pie Face gabbled. Dennis grabbed him by the collar.

"Which way did I go?" he bellowed.

"Huh?" gasped Pie Face.

"You just walked down the street towards... towards..." Curly's lips trembled.

"WELL?" Dennis roared.

"WALTER'S HOUSE!" cried Curly.

Dennis fell back in horror.

"My Dennisbot in the hands of Walter the Softy?" he groaned. "I've gotta get him back! Come on!"

They ran down towards Walter's house. The Colonel was striding towards them. But instead of the frown that usually crossed his face when he saw Dennis, a huge smile spread over his face. He ruffled Dennis's hair.

"There's a good lad. Would you like some more soldiers to play with?"

Dennis could hardly believe his ears!

"I don't play with soppy soldiers!" he bawled.

"Ho-ho, I know that menacing is just a disguise!" chuckled the Colonel. "We've had a lovely time playing soldiers!"

Curly and Pie Face stared at Dennis in amazement.

"NO!" Dennis exclaimed.

Bea squirmed under Dennis's arm.

"See you later at the doll's tea party!" said the Colonel, and he marched away, saluting two garden gnomes.

"What's going on?" asked Curly.

"IT'S NOT ME!" Dennis roared. "It's the Dennisbot! It's all gone wrong! Come on, we've gotta find it!"

They charged down the pavement and slammed into Sergeant Slipper, whose hat fell down over his eyes.

But instead of shouting, Sergeant Slipper CHUCKLED.

"Hello young man," he said. "In a hurry to help some more little old ladies, are you?"

"Little old ladies?" chuckled Pie Face.

"He's been helping them across the street, and rescuing kittens," said Sergeant Slipper happily. "I'm glad to see you've turned over a new leaf, my boy!"

He walked away and Dennis felt sweat pop out on his forehead.

"I feel sick," he said.

"That Dennisbot is wrecking my reputation! It's gotta be stopped!"

Dennis raced through Beanotown with Gnasher in the lead and Bea in his hands, searching for the Dennisbot. Curly and Pie Face followed him at top speed. But everywhere Dennis went, it seemed the Dennisbot had been there first.

"Thank you for teaching my daughter how to skip!" called a mother from across the street.

"Tomorrow I'll show you how to make a bouquet!" said the florist as they ran past his shop.

"You can be the angel in the church play!" said the vicar, who was standing outside the grocer's.

"I hope you like the pink wool for your knitting!" called the lady who owned the wool shop. Dennis stopped dead in his tracks so suddenly that the others crashed into him and fell on the ground in a heap.

"Knitting?" Dennis repeated, through gritted teeth.

"KNITTING!"

Suddenly, Pie Face and Curly gasped. Bea squealed, and Gnasher covered his eyes with his paws. Something hideous and terrifying was skipping towards them. Something so dreadful and unbelievable that heads were turning in the street. Dennis staggered backwards and leaned against a wall.

"It's a nightmare!" he groaned. "Please let it be a nightmare!"

The Dennisbot had lost its black-and-red jumper. Instead, it was wearing a fluffy cardigan. Its hair was neatly slicked down. Its fingernails were clean and neatly cut. Its bootlaces were tied in double knots. But worst of all – worse than wearing a fluffy cardie, worse than skipping, worse than neat hair – he was arm in arm with WALTER THE SOFTY!

"STOP!" Dennis bellowed.

Walter the Softy and the Dennisbot stopped.

"What have you done, you rotten softy?"

"I saw that your robot was switched to 'training', Walter smirked. "I thought someone should show him the *nice* way to behave."

"How do you do?" said the Dennisbot, sticking out its hand. "Would you like to play teddy bears with me?"

"Stop that!" Dennis roared in horror. "Let go of my Dennisbot, softy features, or you'll be sorry!"

"Tee hee!" giggled Walter, taking his arm out of the Dennisbot's. "You're already too late! He knows how to be polite, how to tidy his room and how to knit a cardigan! He knows how to make *a nice cup of tea*!"

"How could anybody sink so low?" said Curly, shaking his head.

Walter skipped away and the Dennisbot waved goodbye to him.

"Do you want to be my friend?" asked the Dennisbot with a soppy grin.

"Not right now," said Dennis, grimly. He walked around to the back of the Dennisbot and reached into his pocket. Then he gave a loud groan.

"The key! I left it on the kitchen table!"

"Shall we have a dolls' tea party?" asked the Dennisbot.

"Shut up," said Curly. "Let's head over to your house and find the key – quick!"

They grabbed the Dennisbot and raced back across town to Dennis's house. It took quite a long time, because the Dennisbot kept stopping to admire flowers, pick up litter and do good deeds.

"*Enough*!" Dennis croaked in horror, as the Dennisbot tried to join in a game of hopscotch with a little girl. He dragged the Dennisbot up the garden path to the back door, closely followed by Pie Face and Curly.

Mum had been cooking all afternoon. She had baked fifty pies, and she had gone upstairs to have a rest and a chocolate éclair. She had left the pies to cool on wire trays, and that was her big mistake. The smell wafted out of the kitchen door and up Pie Face's nose.

"Ahhh," he sighed happily.

There was a note on top of the freshly baked pies.

Dennis put Bea in the sink and looked around the kitchen, trying to spot the key. All the surfaces were clean. There was not a key in sight. A smile spread slowly over his face.

"You know what?" he said to his friends. "I must've left that key on the table where Mum was baking her pies. I reckon Mum must've baked it into a pie."

Pie Face's eyes lit up. He licked his lips.

"There's only one way to find out," he said.

"Everyone grab a pie," said Dennis. "You too, Bea! Find that key!"

"Isn't this a bit...naughty?" asked the Dennisbot.

"Quiet!" Dennis ordered, outraged. "Stand in the corner! Everyone else, get hunting Three, two, one, GO!"

Dennis, Curly and Pie Face dived into the pile of pies and started munching and chomping through them, searching for the key to the Dennisbot. The mound of pies went down, the size of their stomachs went up, and the air was filled with burps and belches. But NO KEY!

Finally, there was just one pie left. Dennis, Curly and Pie Face were draped across the kitchen table, so full of pie that they couldn't speak. It was all up to Bea. She crawled out of the sink and took the last pie in both hands. Then she opened her mouth and took an ENORMOUS bite.

CLUNK!

"Key!" Bea yelled, quickly swallowing the rest of the pie. Dennis leapt to his feet and grabbed the key out of her sticky hands.

"At last!" he cried.

Dennis pushed the key into the Dennisbot's back and switched it to 'Menace'. There was a loud clicking, groaning, wheezing sound. Then the Dennisbot groaned.

"Where's my knitting?" it whimpered. "What shall I do?"

"Get menacing!" Dennis cried eagerly. "Catapults and whoopee cushions! Peashooters and stink bombs! Release your inner menace!"

But the Dennisbot's knees started to knock with a loud, metallic clank-clanking sound.

"Just give me a teddy and a nice cup of tea!" it sobbed.

Dennis stared at the Dennisbot. He stared at his friends. He stared at the empty pie trays scattered around the kitchen. Then a huge grin spread over his face.

"I should have known the Dennisbot wouldn't work," he said.

He turned the key in the Dennisbot's back to 'off'.

"There's no way that a robot could be a menace like me!" he explained. "This Dennisbot belongs in the garage with all the rest of the junk."

"But what about doing double the menacing?" asked Curly, giving a loud burp.

"I can do triple the menacing if I want!" Dennis grinned. "It's best to leave the menacing up to the best real-life menace in the world!"

Just then, they heard Mum coming down the stairs.

"I'm just going to check on my pies," she called to Dad.

Dennis, Bea, Curly and Pie Face exchanged glances. Then Dennis stuffed Bea under his arm and grabbed the Dennisbot.

"Time to shove this Dennisbot in the garage and get outta here!" he yelled happily. "SCARPER!"

THE ULTIMATE MENACE

"What are they DOING?" hissed Curly in amazement.

They were hiding behind a hedge in the park. They had been crawling through the undergrowth, minding their own business (on their way to ambush Minnie the Minx with a bag of water bombs), when they heard a REALLY bad impression of a trumpet. It was Walter the Softy, and he was playing with his friends Spotty Perkins and Bertie Blenkinsop. They were 'galloping' around the park on hobby horses, with ribbons tied around their arms, wearing pink tunics and soppy expressions.

"They *think* they're playing knights!" snorted Dennis, clamping his hand over Pie Face's mouth to stop him chortling.

"Excuse me, Sir Prancealot, would you like to come to tea at the beautiful and romantic castle of Camelot?" they heard Bertie call to Walter.

"Sir Prancealot?" spluttered Curly.

"Oh rather, how simply delightful," drawled Walter. "Thank you, Sir Frolicforth!"

"Oh I can't wait to reach the castle!" cried Spotty, clasping his hands together (and nearly dropping his horse).

"I hear that all the most beautiful maidens are going to be there."

"That's true, Sir Nimbletoes," said Walter, "but the most beautiful of them all is my coochy-woochy Lady Matilda!"

From behind the hedge they bowed to each other, mimicking

the softies. Pie Face laughed so hard that tears ran down his face.

"If they're knights, where are their swords?" asked Curly.

"These are SOFTIES, you brain donor," said Dennis. "They'd faint if they had to hold a sword!"

Curly catapulted a spare water bomb at Dennis and they had a quick and silent fight.

"Okay!" puffed Curly, when Dennis had pinned him down. "But what are we gonna do about these softies?"

"It can't be allowed to go on!" said Dennis. "Softies playing knights?

What next? Sergeant Slipper being promoted? The Colonel finding his marbles? No way! We've gotta do something – right now!"

"GNASH!" agreed Gnasher, who was nipping at Pie Face's rucksack (there were several pies in there).

"Yeah!" said Curly. "If they're gonna play Camelot, they need to be shown *how*!"

"They need bows and arrows!" said Dennis, with a grin.

"Shields!" cried Pie Face.

"Swords!" added Curly.

They stashed the bag of water bombs under a hedge for later.

"Right, men," said Dennis. "You know what's ahead of us. It's a tough job, but somebody's gotta do it! It's time to teach these softies how to *really* play knights of the round table!"

Dennis and Gnasher raced around the park, collecting branches, stones and squirrels (Gnasher). Pie Face ran back to his street to gather all the weapons he could find. Curly darted home and borrowed most of his mum's saucepans and baking trays, and ALL his dad's belts. The three menaces met up again fifteen minutes later. Curly strapped the pans and trays to them all with his dad's belts (Gnasher got a milk pan on his head). Then Pie Face armed them with bows and arrows, swords and shields.

"And now for the finishing touch!" Dennis chuckled. He showed them a small, moveable fort that he had made from sticks and branches and leaves he'd found in the park. They could get inside it and move it along from the inside!

"Awesome!" gasped Curly.

"We're not worthy!" added Pie Face. "You're the ultimate menace!"

"Yeah, I know," said Dennis, modestly. "But there's one more thing we need!"

"What's that?" asked Curly.

"The ultimate menace has to have the ultimate weapon!" said Dennis. He pulled a pair of his dad's braces out of his pocket and tied them to a thick log that stuck up in the middle of the fort's battlements.

"It's a giant catapult!" Curly chortled. "Excellent!"

Dennis placed a massive stink bomb in the sling.

"Armed and ready!" he said. "ATTACK!"

They raced towards the softies, who were in the middle of a picnic with Matilda and a bunch of dollies.

"Release!" cried Dennis.

The stink bomb hurtled through the air and landed with a loud, smelly splash... all over Matilda's head!

"UGH! What a pong!" cried the softies, leaping to their feet.

Then Dennis, Curly and Pie Face charged into view, waving their weapons and whooping.

"We charge you in the name of the Fort of the Menaces!" Dennis roared. "Draw your swords and fight to the death!"

"EEK!" squeaked Bertie, diving behind Matilda.

"My beautiful dress! My silky hair! It's all ruined!" Matilda wailed.

"Don't be such a drama queen!" Spotty sobbed. "What about MEEEEE? I'm scared of catapults! I'm scared of bows and arrows! WAHHHH!"

"Go away and leave us alone!" Walter hissed, his knees knocking together like coconut shells. "You don't know anything about knights!"

"Oh yeah?" grinned Dennis. He looked at Bertie's quivering

bottom, which was sticking out from behind Matilda. "I reckon I know loads about being a knight, softy breath! Knights used to go around firing arrows to save ladies in distress…"

He fired a sucker arrow at Bertie's bottom.

"YEEEAAOOOWWCCHHH!" squealed Bertie, springing three feet into the air. He started running before he touched the ground, and in a flash he had raced off to the other side of the park.

"…they set their trusty steeds on their enemies…"

Gnasher bounded over to where Spotty was trying to climb a tree and pulled him down by one of his pink-

and-blue spotted socks. Spotty howled and stumbled off after Bertie, dragging his hobby horse behind him.

"...and they challenge each other to duels!" Dennis finished, drawing his sword. He advanced on Walter with a battling glint in his eye. Walter threw up his hands, flung his hobby horse into the bushes and ran off, raising a cloud of dust behind him. "Hang on!" Dennis bellowed. "I hadn't got to the part about the round table yet!"

The menaces guffawed as the screams of the softies faded into the distance.

"Aw, shame," said Curly, wiping his streaming eyes. "Where have they got to?"

"You menaces are going to be really sorry for being so mean to my darling Walter!" said a pinched voice.

They turned around and had to cover their noses as Matilda stepped towards them.

"Well, *you're* gonna be really sorry if you don't have a bath soon," Pie Face chuckled. "Yeah," said Curly.

"Walter won't come near you if you smell like that! It might hurt his delicate nosie!"

Matilda stuck out her tongue at them and stormed off.

"Come on," said Curly. "Let's pick up those water bombs and go to find Minnie."

"Nah," said Pie Face. "I reckon it's about time for a little snack. Let's go to Pies-R-Us!"

"No," said Dennis. "I think we should head across to the other side of the park. I reckon those softies could do with a few more lessons in courtly manners!"

The menaces raced over to the play park. The softies were there.

"What are they doing in the play park?" asked Curly. "It's for toddlers! Even Bea thinks she's too old for it!"

They crept closer and saw the softies on board the toy wooden boat that stood in the middle of the play park. Each of them was wearing a captain's hat and a neckerchief.

"Oooh, I hope I don't get seasick!" simpered Bertie.

"No danger of that," smirked Walter. "This is all the fun of yachting without any of the scary things that go with it, like water, and fish…"

"… and wind…" added Spotty.

"… and motors…" said Bertie.

"… AND PIRATES!" Dennis yelled, as he and the other two menaces hurtled over the low fence into the play park. "Avast, you scurvy-swabs! You'll be walking the gangplank before you're an hour older, you landlubbers!"

Dennis had found an old newspaper and folded it into a pirate's hat. Curly had torn of a section of Pie Face's trousers (when he was busy eating a pie) and had been drawing on it in white chalk. Now he attached it to a branch and waved it in the air.

"The skull and crossbones rules the ocean waves!" he bellowed. "The Jolly Roger is coming to teach you what being at sea is all about!"

"Prepare the cannonballs!" Dennis yelled.

Pie Face ran to fetch the enormous catapult Dennis had built, while Curly sniffed out a box of rotten tomatoes that someone had thrown away.

"I want my mumsy!" wailed Bertie, as a single, squashy, rotten tomato sailed through the air and landed on his hat with a PLOP.

"Leave here at once, Dennis!" Walter said, waggling a limp finger at the pirates. "We're playing yachts and it's none of your business!"

Dennis just gave him a wide, wide grin.

"FIRE!" he bawled.

The air was filled with rotten tomatoes! They crashed and splashed on the deck, on the masts, and most of all on the softies. Then Dennis gave a loud whistle, and dozens of birds came dive bombing out of the sky, landing all over the ship and eagerly pecking up all the tomato remains. The softies crouched on the deck with their arms over their heads

"Excellent!" grinned Dennis. "The birds know that wherever I am, there's gonna be food! They're our pirate parrots! Come on, men! Board the enemy vessel!"

Dennis, Curly and Pie Face swarmed up the side of the boat and jumped on deck with loud, piratical chuckles.

"You're for the plank!" Dennis chuckled. "Unless, of course, you join our pirate gang!"

"Certainly not!" sniffed Walter.

"I don't like it!" wailed Bertie. "I don't want to be a pirate!"

"I was hoping you'd say that!" said Dennis, rubbing his hands together. "Curly, set up the gang plank!"

Curly dragged a trampoline under the gangplank, while Curly lined the softies up.

"Ready!" they called out.

"Now, walk the plank, soppy softies!" Dennis cried.

"I'm not jumping off there!" Spotty squeaked.

"My mumsy told me never to jump off anything higher than my potty!" said Bertie.

"I might get my shorts dirty!" yowled Walter.

"Put it this way, me hearties," Dennis said. "Either you walk the plank...or you face my very own sea monster!"

Gnasher gave a loud GNASH and bared his teeth in his most piratical way.

"Oo-er!" Walter cried. "Jump!"

"I can't!" sobbed Bertie.

"Just close your eyes and think of teddies!" Walter squealed, as he stepped off the gangplank, bounced off the trampoline and hurtled into the bushes beside the play park.

"I don't like trampoleeeennnsss!" whined Bertie as he whizzed through the air after Walter.

"I want my cuddly hot water bottle!" Spotty moaned, as he followed his softy friends.

"Victory!" cheered the three menaces. "Raise the flag!"

"This calls for a celebration!" said Dennis.

"Pies!" cried Pie Face.

"Sausages!" gnashed Gnasher.

"DADS!" hollered Curly.

"We don't want our dads at a pirate celebration, you nutter!" said Dennis, bewildered.

"Too bad!" chorused three voices.

Dennis and Pie Face looked where Curly was pointing. Their dads were standing beside the ship with their hands behind their backs. Matilda was watching them with her arms folded. She was wearing a smug expression that Dennis didn't like AT ALL.

"You pack of menaces have been causing all sorts of trouble today," said Dennis's dad.

"Taking all my belts," said Curly's dad (he was keeping his trousers up with one of Curly's mum's headscarves).

"Disturbing softies," said Pie Face's dad.

"They were already disturbed!" claimed Dennis, fuming.

"We were only playing pirates!" said Curly, innocently.

"Really," said Dennis's dad, with a worrying smile. "Well if you're such great pirates, there's one thing you're missing…"

"What's that?" said Pie Face.

"WATER!" yelled the dads, pulling three hoses from behind their backs. The menaces and Gnasher were thrown backwards by three jets of water! Spluttering, coughing and soaked to the skin, they scrambled down the other side of the ship and raced out of the play park and over to the safety of the woods.

Dennis, Pie Face and Curly pulled off their jumpers and wrung the water out of them. Gnasher shook himself so hard that his fur stood out even more than usual.

"What a dirty trick!" Pie Face exclaimed, as soon as he had got his breath back.

"Never mind," chuckled Curly. "We've had a top menacing day! We've stormed the knights of Camelot and made them walk the plank!"

"And even if we're soaking now," added Dennis, "we'll never be half as wet as those soppy softies!"

CALAMITY COLONEL

"It's not fair!" bellowed Dennis.

"No no no no no!" Bea clamoured, banging her rattle on Dad's head.

"You've already been out *once* this year!" Dennis roared. "What more do you want?"

"Er, we don't *have* to go if you don't want us to," said Dad. He was feeling very silly in his spotted bow tie and purple tuxedo, and didn't really want anyone to see him.

"I've been looking forward to this dance for a month!" said Mum, with a dangerous glint in her eye. "If we don't go, there'll be TROUBLE!"

Dad looked at Dennis.

"You're going to be babysat by the Colonel, and that's the end of it!"

Mum and Dad marched off down the garden path as the Colonel walked up, wearing his thickest tin hat.

"Thank you for taking this on, Colonel," said Mum. "There aren't many people brave enough."

"You mean there aren't many people *mad* enough," said Dad under his breath.

He glanced at Dennis, who was standing in the doorway with a face like thunder.

"I think we should go while the going's good," he said in Mum's ear.

Dennis scowled and stomped upstairs to find his extra-large peashooter. The Colonel strode into the house, patted Bea on the head and got a handful of chewing gum.

"No more of that or I'll put you in solitary!" he barked. Bea looked up at him, narrowed her eyes and bit him.

"YEEEOOOWWLL!" screeched the Colonel, hopping around the hallway. "Steady! That is not how young ladies behave!"

"NOT!" Bea roared, hurling her rattle at the Colonel. It clanged on his tin hat and bounced off to land on Gnasher's head.

"GNASH!" snapped Gnasher, nipping the Colonel's other ankle.

"ARGHH! By jove! That's it! You're both going in solitary confinement!" blustered the Colonel. He stuffed Bea under one arm and Gnasher under the other.

When Dennis came downstairs, his pockets bristling with weapons, the house was strangely quiet. The Colonel was in the kitchen, lining up his favourite soldiers on the table.

"Harrummph! AttenSHUN!" he cried. "We are here to guard this house against pilferers, pickpockets and pranksters!"

"Good luck!" chortled Dennis, firing a stream of paper darts with his peashooter. The Colonel turned brick red and charged at Dennis, who dived out of the way and crash-landed on Mum's telephone table.

"Hey, where's Gnasher?" asked Dennis, realising that no one was biting the Colonel's ankles. "Where's Bea?"

"SOLITARY CONFINEMENT!" bellowed the Colonel in his best parade ground voice, as steam came out of his nostrils. "And that's just where you're going, my lad!"

He pulled out a telescopic grabber and snared Dennis's jumper.

"I call this my 'menace menacer'!" said the Colonel, pushing Dennis up the stairs. "I had to use it on the SAS once. I can babysit all you rotten kids without having to lay one finger on you!"

"Hmmm, I can feel a plan hatching," said Dennis. He let the Colonel push him into his room and lock the door.

"That'll teach you!" the Colonel bellowed through the door.

"Oho," laughed Dennis quietly. "It's not *me* who's gonna be learning a lesson!"

As the Colonel marched downstairs, Dennis peered out of the window. The garden shed was shaking on its foundations. "I think I've found Gnasher!" Dennis chuckled. He pulled his spare grappling hook and rope from under his bed, tied it around his waist and fixed the other end to a bed leg. Then he fed the line out and clambered onto the window ledge. He leaned across to Bea's window and looked in. Bea was standing up in her cot, gnawing the bars. She grinned when she saw Dennis.

"Revenge!" Dennis bellowed at her through the window.

"SWEET!" Bea babbled.

Dennis used the rope to walk down the side of the house and sped across to the shed.

"Freedom!" he roared, opening the shed door. Gnasher burst out, hungry

for the Colonel's ankles. They raced up to the house and pressed their noses against the sitting-room window.

The Colonel had just settled down in front of his third-favourite programme about soldiers. He had Dennis's biscuit jar beside him and he was wearing Mum's foot warmer.

"HUH! Lucky my biscuit jar is empty!" said Dennis. "Come on, Gnasher, let's get this revenge on the road!"

Gnasher gave a loud gnashing bark and the Colonel turned and saw them. He let out a bellow of rage, leapt to his feet and fell smack on his face because of the foot warmer.

"SCARPER!" Dennis hollered. They flew out of the garden and down the street, just as it started to get dark. Behind them they heard the front door open and the Colonel's army boots pounding along the pavement.

"Through the back gardens!" Dennis told Gnasher, vaulting over a fence.

They sped through the gardens, but the Colonel was close behind them. Up ahead, Curly's mum's washing line was filled with white sheets. Dennis and Gnasher ducked under them, but the Colonel ran straight into them and got two sheets wound around him. The back door opened and Curly's mum came out with the broom. She saw the Colonel in the twilight, waving his arms around under the sheets, and gave an ear-piercing SCREAM!

"Don't be alarmed, Madam!" the Colonel spluttered, pulling the sheets off and giving her a low bow. "It is I! I was just—"

"Colonel!" shrieked Curly's mum. "I suppose you think that's funny! Ruining my sheets and scaring me out of my wits! I'll teach you a thing or two about being scared!"

She picked up her broom and charged at him as Dennis and Gnasher ran off, chortling.

"Retreat!" yelled the Colonel in his cowardly fashion.

"That's the Colonel's first lesson!" Dennis told Gnasher. "Come on, we need to go to the den!"

They raced over to Dennis's secret den to pick up some extra supplies. Then they crept out into the street again and strolled along in the glow from the streetlamps. Dennis shoved his hands in his pockets and started whistling, his eyes darting from left to right. Eventually, when he was outside Walter's house, he heard a roar. The Colonel was bounding towards them, with one of Curly's mum's sheets still trailing behind him.

"Timing is everything," Dennis grinned. He pulled a handful of stink pellets from his pocket and looked up at Walter's open bedroom window. Just at the right moment, he threw the pellets into Walter's room and dived behind a rose bush in the front garden. The Colonel skidded to a halt and glowered at the rose bush.

"Don't think I didn't see where you went!" he bawled. "Just you wait—"

"EEEEKKK! MUMSY!" warbled a voice. Walter and his mumsy appeared at the bedroom window. When she saw the Colonel, Walter's mumsy was so furious that her curlers popped off her head.

"What do you mean by throwing stink pellets at my darling boy?" she squealed. "You could have done terrible damage to his sweet little nose!"

"My dear lady, it wasn't—"

"NO EXCUSES! Just stay right where you are!"

"That's our cue!" Dennis whispered in glee, as Walter and his mumsy disappeared from the window. He and Gnasher darted out from behind the rose bush and made a run for it. The Colonel started to chase them again, and Dennis led him on, ploughing through rose bushes and flower beds, splashing through ponds and smashing through gnomes. Lights went on all down the street and doors and windows were flung open, just in time to see the Colonel speeding past.

"It's the Colonel!" the neighbours cried.

"He's finally flipped!"

"Just wait till I get my hands on him!"

"My beautiful gnomes!"

But nothing could stop the Colonel. Dennis led him into Beanotown, zooming through the streets and keeping his head down. The Colonel stomped after him like an angry elephant, weaving across roads and in front of lorries and cars. The air was filled with the sound of screeching brakes and angry motorists. Sergeant Slipper heard the

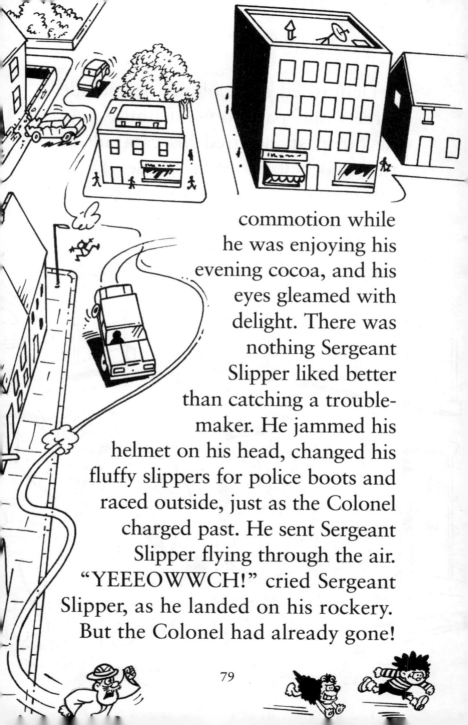

commotion while he was enjoying his evening cocoa, and his eyes gleamed with delight. There was nothing Sergeant Slipper liked better than catching a trouble-maker. He jammed his helmet on his head, changed his fluffy slippers for police boots and raced outside, just as the Colonel charged past. He sent Sergeant Slipper flying through the air. "YEEEOWWCH!" cried Sergeant Slipper, as he landed on his rockery. But the Colonel had already gone!

Dennis led the Colonel down side streets and past rows of houses. As he ran past, he fired his catapult at the doorbell of each house. Door after door opened and saw the Colonel running past!

"Think that's funny, do you?" they shouted. "Grow up, Colonel!"

Dennis put on an extra burst of speed and darted down the path that led to the river. He pelted along the river bank until he saw the night anglers, sitting in a row along the bank, with their fishing lines in the water. Dennis and Gnasher tiptoed into hiding behind a bush and waited. Soon, the Colonel came along, puffing and yelling.

"Come out, you little menace! I'll make you march ten miles! Disobedience in the ranks!"

"Quiet!" hissed the fishermen furiously. The Colonel hadn't even seen them there. He jumped out of his skin and fell against one of them, who shoved him back. SPLASH! The Colonel fell into the river!

"Come on, Gnasher!" Dennis hissed.

They jogged back home and raced upstairs. Dennis opened Bea's door and gave her a wink.

"Mission accomplished!" he chortled. "Your turn!"

Bea chuckled, then opened her mouth...

"WAHHHHHHHHH!"

Dennis closed the door, went to his room and peered out of the window. Mum and Dad were just walking through the front gate.

"Just in time," Dennis said with a grin.

He leapt into bed and Gnasher flopped on top of the covers.

Downstairs, Mum and Dad opened the front door.

"Colonel? Where are you?" called Mum.

They went upstairs and looked into Dennis's room.

"Dennis and Gnasher are asleep," said Mum in surprise. "Ah, they're so sweet when they're sleeping."

"Yeeess," said Dad, very doubtfully. "Yuck," Dennis muttered to himself, very quietly. Mum and Dad opened Bea's door, and she stopped screaming at once. "Good girl," said Dad.

They went downstairs again.

"Where on earth can the Colonel be?" asked Dad.

"Right here!" puffed a voice. They turned around and Mum gave a small scream. The Colonel was standing in the doorway, panting. His clothes were sopping wet and filled with brambles and leaves. He still had part of Curly's mum's sheet wrapped around him. His face was muddy and riverweed was hanging down from his helmet.

"What *have* you been doing?" gasped Dad.

"I've been chasing that wretched menace of yours all round Beanotown!" seethed the Colonel. "Your children are monsters! Your daughter tried to bite my legs off!"

"Colonel, I'm surprised at you!" said Mum, crossly. "Dennis is fast asleep, and Bea is being a very good little girl (for once)! What has got into you?"

"I'll tell you what's got into him," said Curly's mum, marching up the path. "He's been playing ghosts and trying to scare people half to death!"

A crowd of people was behind her, looking very VERY cross.

"He's been throwing stink pellets at my little angel!"

"He's been causing traffic jams all across town!"

"Ringing doorbells and running away!"

"Wrecking gardens!"

"Scaring the fish!"

"He's a complete fruitloop!" said the man whose gnomes had been smashed.

"And he's going to be sorry!" added Sergeant Slipper, eyeing the colonel suspiciously.

"IT WASN'T ME!" roared the Colonel. "IT WAS THAT… THAT… THAT CATAPULT - WAVING, STINK - BOMB - CARRYING PAIN IN THE NECK!"

"Well, really," huffed Mum. "Blaming my boy when he's fast asleep!"

"It was you we saw!" said Sergeant Slipper. "Not Dennis!"

"WE WANT COMPENSATION!"
yelled the crowd. The Colonel pulled
off his tin hat and stamped on it.
Upstairs, Dennis quietly closed his
bedroom window and grinned at
Gnasher.

"I think the Colonel's learnt his lesson at last!" he chortled. "He won't be babysitting us again in a hurry!"

More Bumper BEANObooks fun...

1-84539-202-7

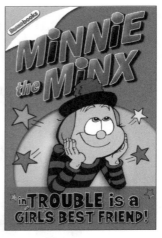

1-84539-203-5

1-84539-095-4

1-84539-096-2

... make sure you've got them all!

1-84539-097-0

1-84539-098-9

1-84539-204-3

1-84539-205-1

YOU'LL MEET...

...EVERY WEEK IN

Written by RACHEL ELLIOT

Illustrated by BARRIE APPLEBY

published under licence by

185 Fleet Street, London, EC4A 2HS

THE
UNFOLDING

A.M. Homes

GRANTA

Granta Publications, 12 Addison Avenue, London W11 4QR

First published in Great Britain by Granta Books, 2022
This paperback edition published by Granta Books, 2023
Originally published in the United States in 2022 by Viking,
an imprint of Penguin Random House, New York

A CIP catalogue record for this book is available from the British Library.

1 3 5 7 9 10 8 6 4 2

ISBN 978 1 78378 535 3 (paperback)
ISBN 978 1 78378 534 6 (ebook)

Offset by Avon DataSet Ltd, Alcester, Warwickshire

Printed and bound by CPI Group (UK) Ltd, Croydon, CR0 4YY

www.granta.com